Based on the original script by Andrew Brenner
Illustrated by Tommy Stubbs

A GOLDEN BOOK · NEW YORK

Thomas the Tank Engine & Friends™

CREATED BY BRITT ALLCROFT

Based on The Railway Series by The Reverend W Awdry.
© 2018 Gullane (Thomas) LLC. Thomas the Tank Engine & Friends and Thomas & Friends are trademarks of Gullane (Thomas) Limited.
© HIT Entertainment Limited. HIT and the HIT logo are trademarks of HIT Entertainment Limited.
All rights reserved. Published in the United States by Golden Books, an imprint of Random House Children's Books, a division of Penguin Random House
LLC, 1745 Broadway, New York, NY 10019, and in Canada by Penguin Random House Canada Limited, Toronto. Golden Books, A Golden Book,
A Little Golden Book, the G colophon, and the distinctive gold spine are registered trademarks of Penguin Random House LLC.
rhcbooks.com   www.thomasandfriends.com
ISBN 978-1-5247-7316-8
Printed in the United States of America
10 9 8 7 6 5 4 3 2 1
Random House Children's Books supports the First Amendment and celebrates the right to read.

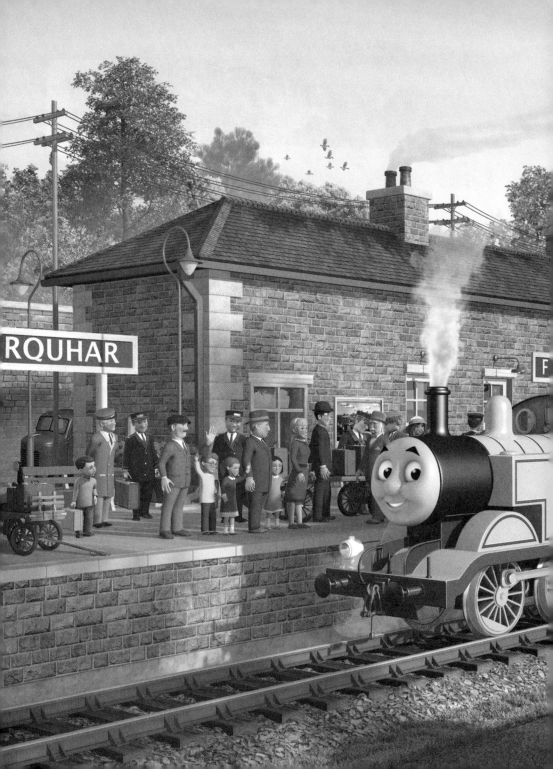

It was a sunny day on the Island of Sodor. Thomas the Tank Engine was excited to meet a race car named Ace. He was in a round-the-world rally, speeding through five continents.

"I've always wanted to see the world," Thomas peeped.

"You should do it," replied Ace. "You could be the first railway engine to go all the way around the world."

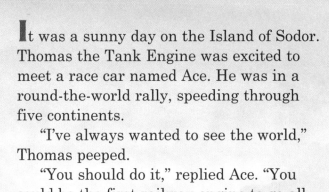

The next day, Thomas and Ace set sail for the
first continent, Africa. After that, they would go
on to South America, North America, Asia, and,
finally, back to Sodor through Europe.

When they arrived in Africa, Ace left—without Thomas! He sped to a city called Dar es Salaam, in Tanzania, but Thomas had to stick to the rails.

A Yard Manager gave Thomas lots of trucks to deliver to the faraway city. The little engine set off all by himself.

It was hard work pulling the trucks up the big hills. Luckily, Thomas met an engine named Nia, who offered to help. "Two engines are much better than one," she peeped. Thomas replied that he didn't need help.

But Thomas did need help. The trucks were too heavy for him to pull alone. Nia stayed with Thomas and helped him with his heavy trucks.

Nia also helped when they met a giant
elephant blocking the tracks.

She and the trucks sang a lullaby,
and the elephant wandered off to nap
beneath a tree.

Nia traveled with Thomas all the way to Dar es Salaam.
"Please keep your eyes open for my friend Ace," Thomas peeped.
Nia's friend Kwaku said he had seen some race cars, but they
had left.
"Ace must have gone on without me again," said Thomas.
"He doesn't sound like a very good friend," said Nia.

Thomas knew Ace's next race was in Rio de Janeiro, in South America. Nia asked if she could help Thomas find Ace, but he told her to go home. Then he steamed to the Docks and was loaded onto a ship to continue on his big adventure.

At sea, Thomas was surprised to find Nia on the ship. She wanted to travel with him and be the *second* engine to go all the way around the world.

Thomas was also surprised to find Ace was on board, too!

"Why didn't you wait for me?" Thomas asked the yellow race car.

"You want to be a free spirit, don't you?" Ace asked.

When they reached South America, Ace sped off— and left Thomas alone again!

Thomas wanted to follow Ace across South America to the next rally, in North America. Luckily, a railway worker needed Thomas to carry coffee to San Francisco, in the United States.

Nia offered to help, and they set off together through the rain forest, pulling the heavy load.

On the way, they found Ace. He had an accident while racing, so they loaded him up and gave him a ride.

When they reached North America, Ace didn't want to go to San Francisco. He wanted Thomas to take him to the Salt Flats in Utah so he could get repaired and meet the other racers.

Ace convinced Thomas to play a trick on Nia, and they sped off without her.

Ace told Thomas to race across the western lands. Thomas went so fast, he came off the track!

An old mining engine called Beau and his friends got Thomas back on the rails. As everyone worked together to help, Thomas realized he'd done a terrible thing to Nia.

"We should have stayed with her," he peeped. "It wasn't nice to play a trick on her."

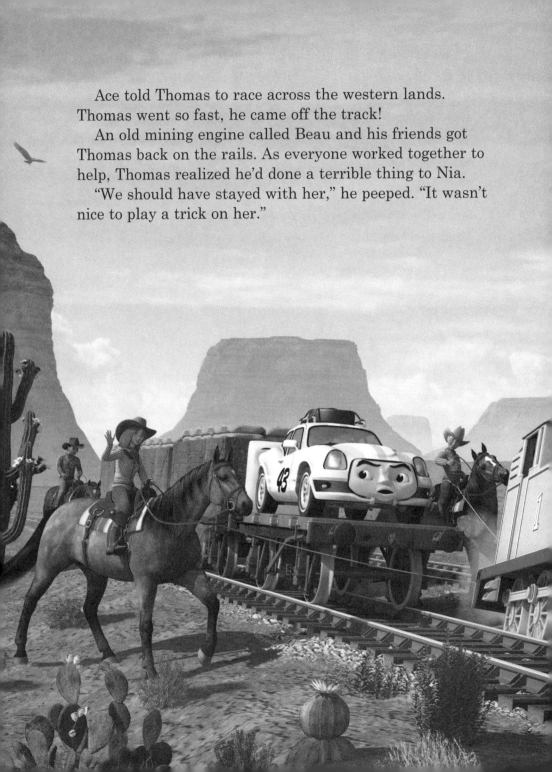

At the salt flats, Ace met up with the
other racers. But Thomas wanted to deliver
his coffee and find Nia to apologize.

He steamed on to San Francisco with his
load. But Nia was not there. Thomas hoped
he could find her at the next stop: China.

Thomas found Nia—on a snowy mountain in China!
"I'm sorry! I wish I hadn't upset you. Can we still be
friends?" he peeped.

But before Nia could respond, there was an avalanche!
It hit Nia and knocked her off the tracks. Thomas was
too small to pull her back onto the rails by himself.

Just then, a Chinese engine named Yong Bao came crashing through the snow! His big plow cleared the way, and he pulled both engines to safety!

Thomas thanked Yong Bao for being big and strong.

"We're bigger and stronger—when we work together," said Nia.

"So where are you going now?" asked Yong Bao.

"Continent number five—Europe!" said Thomas and Nia.

Thomas and Nia then set off for Europe—and the Island of Sodor.

Thomas introduced Nia to Emily, Percy, James, Henry, Edward, and Gordon. His friends steamed with happiness to see the two engines who had traveled on a big world adventure!